Title: The Am

Adventure

Ha

Shark Encounter

By Greg Hibbins

Dedication

This book is dedicated to all teachers.
You work so hard to give children
one of the greatest gifts of all,
a love of learning, as well the tools they will
need to be successful in life.

Never grow weary of passing this wonderful
gift onto children.

Table of Contents

Prologue

The two boys featured in this series of stories are Solly, short for Solomon, and Harry. They are eight years old and are ethnic Capetonians, living in Cape Town, South Africa. The two boys are always up to mischief and have many adventures together. There will be thirty books in total in the 'Adventures of Solly and Harry Series'. The full set should be completed by mid-2016.

There is a free audio file that goes with this book, and it is available as a free download once the book has been purchased. The link is at the end of the book.

At the end of each book, Solly and Harry journal all they have learnt on their adventure. This journal is a great tool for discussion, with parents, to reinforce good values and lessons that will equip the reader for life.

Chapter 1: The Adventure Begins

The sun was just coming up over the water. The city of Cape Town looked so beautiful in the early morning light.

Down on the narrow road there were signs of early movement, as an eight-year-old boy ran at full speed up the road. Arriving at his friend's house, he threw open the gate and rushed up to the front door. He started banging on the door and shouting out at the top of his voice, "Harry, Harry, come on. Open the door!"

This was followed by another furious bout of banging with his fists on the door. About a minute and a half later, the door flew open to reveal another little boy, also eight years old. Eyes encrusted with sleep, he looked at his friend and said, "Solly, what are you doing here so early? The sun is hardly up."

Solly was clearly excited. He said, "Harry, you won't believe it! You won't believe it!"

Harry had been down this road before, so with a grim look on his face he said, "Solly, what won't I believe?"

"Harry, Harry, you won't believe it!" exclaimed Solly again.

Harry knew his friend well. Grabbing him by the shoulders, he gave him a good shake. "Solly, slow down. What won't I believe?"

Solly took a moment to pause, sucked in a deep breath and then said, "My Uncle Frankie... my Uncle Frankie has given us a special surprise!"

That made Harry smile; he loved surprises. Harry loved adventures, and Harry especially loved surprises and adventures with Solly. He and Solly had been on many, many adventures together. Harry asked again, "Solly, what surprise?"

Solly said, "My Uncle Frankie has given us tickets to go shark diving."

A funny look came across Harry's face; he said, "Solly, did I hear you right? Did you say your Uncle Frankie has given us tickets to go shark diving?"

"Yes," said Solly, a look of absolute excitement on his face. Harry didn't have a look of excitement on his face right at that moment; the idea of climbing into water with Great White Sharks was not his idea of fun.

He said, "And you're excited about this? The idea of swimming with Great White Sharks does not scare you? I can tell you for sure that it scares me."

"No; I'm not scared," said Solly. "I am really, really excited."

"Well," said Harry, "I can see that you're excited, but I'm not sure how you can find climbing into water with Great White Sharks that eat seals and people exciting!"

Solly look at his friend with a puzzled look on his face and said, "Harry! How can you not find shark cage diving an exciting adventure?"

"Oh," said Harry. Solly had omitted to mention that one very important word initially – **CAGE**.

Harry knew all about shark cage diving. His daddy and mommy had been on an adventure like that, and he knew Solly's mommy and daddy had been on an adventure like that.

It was a very popular tourist attraction in Cape Town. Tour guides took tourists from all over the world out to sea, stopping just off Seal Island in False Bay. Once there, they would put large metal cages into the water, and the tourists would climb into the cages wearing wetsuits, aqualungs and diving goggles.

The Great White Sharks would swim around the cages, normally because the tour operators had been pouring a mixture of offal and blood into the water. They called the mixture chum.

Tourists were safe in the cages; the sharks could not get to them. But the tourists got to view a great and wonderful creature of the sea, the Great White Shark, up really close and personal.

"That sounds really exciting!" said Harry. "I can't wait. Come on then; we need to practice."

Solly looked across at his friend, a furrow forming on his brow.

"What you mean, Harry? We need to practice? For what?" Solly said.

"I mean we need to practice; we can't go into the cage and make it look like we don't know what we doing! There might be some cool girls there. We don't want them to think we are stupid."

"*Ja*," said Solly. "I knew there would be some girls involved somewhere along the line."

Harry said, "Just wait here. Let me get changed out of my PJ's."

Within three minutes he was back again. Harry said, "Come, Solly!"

Solly followed Harry into his dad's garage. Harry dived into a big cardboard box, much bigger than he was. Solly heard the sounds of Harry rummaging around inside the box, and a few minutes later Harry's head popped over the corner of the box.

"I knew they were in here somewhere," he said, throwing some objects out of the box to land at Solly's feet.

"What are those?" said Solly, looking down at the objects with curiosity.

"Those…" said Harry, quite happy to be the fount of all wisdom from whom the knowledge flowed, "… are diving goggles and diving flippers, and these are snorkels or breathing tubes."

"Oh," said Solly, looking at the slightly old and faded rubber objects with a sense of suspicion.

"Come on," said Harry. "We need to get going!"

"Where are we going?" Solly asked. "The swimming pool?" he ventured to guess.

"No, of course not!" said Harry. "If we go to the swimming pool, we might look stupid. There might even be some girls looking on; I don't want to look stupid in front of them."

"*Ja*," said Solly. "Again with the girl thing. So where are we going to go?"

Harry looked across at his friend said, "Well, I know a place about three kilometres from here with a tidal pool down among the rocks on the beach. We can go and practice in that tidal pool."

A look of dismay and fear came over Solly's face. He said, "*Ja*, I know that tidal pool too, and there are a lot of sharks that swim around it. Just on the other side of that tidal pool is very, very deep water. That's where the seals often come to catch fish and to sunbathe on the rocks. My dad said that it's a very dangerous place, and we must never go swimming there."

"*Ja*," said Harry. "It is dangerous if you're going to swim out in the open water. But we going to the tidal pool; its low tide at the moment, so there will be enough water in the pool for us to swim. It'll be safe for us to practice our snorkelling and scuba diving skills."

"Okay," said Solly reluctantly, feeling a mixture of excitement and apprehension. "But we had better let our parents know."

"Are you crazy? It's Saturday morning; it's still really early. My mom and dad are fast asleep," said Harry.

"Mine too," said Solly.

"If we wake them up on a Saturday morning when they are having their lie in, we will be in big trouble. Also, you know what grown-ups are like! They will try to stop us having fun, so come on! Let's go!"

"Okay," said Solly. "Let's do it."

Chapter 2: Tidal Pool Fun

The boys made their way along the windy road that led down to the tidal pool on the beach.

They laughed and joked and talked about all the great adventures they were going to have when they went shark cage diving. They were really excited when they arrived at the beach; taking off their takkies or trainers, they made their way down to the tidal pool.

The water was crystal clear; they could see the little fish darting about in the water. There were even some bigger fish too, some as long as their arms.

"Look!" said Solly. "There's an octopus swimming in the water."

Sure enough, there was a smallish octopus swimming beautifully in the water, the early morning rays of the sun catching its beautiful action as it made its way gracefully through the water.

The two boys scanned the water very carefully and neither of them could see any danger; there certainly weren't any sharks.

Solly lifted his eyes up from the water of the tidal pool and looked across the shelf of rocks that formed the tidal wall between the pool and the deeper ocean water beyond.

As Solly carefully scanned the deeper water beyond, a huge fin suddenly appeared. A Great White Shark broke the surface as it cruised along, looking for a seal for breakfast.

"Look!" said Solly, his voice rising to a high-pitched squeak as he felt the ripple of fear go down his back.

Harry also glanced out over the water, and there another fin appeared, and then another. The two young boys counted at least four Great White Sharks swimming in the deeper water at the edge of the rock shelf. All of the sharks were on the lookout for a seal or other food source for breakfast.

"Well," said Harry, "we don't have time to watch the sharks today. Soon we will be swimming with them, when we do our shark cage dive. We've got to practice our swimming technique."

The two boys quickly stripped off their clothes and put on swimming trunks. Then, taking the old, faded snorkels, goggles and flippers, they made their way into the tidal pool.

"Wow!" said Solly to Harry. "This water is really, really, really cold."

"Don't worry," said Harry. "Soon we will be warm."

Sure enough, in a few moments the boys were swimming in the lovely, crystal clear water and having lots of fun.

Suddenly, Solly stood up and said, "Harry, I've got a problem. I can't see out of my goggles."

Harry stood up as well and said, "Me, too."

The boys goggles were all steamed up. As the hot air coming out from the boys' noses into the goggles had met the colder glass that had been cooled by the water, this scientific reaction on the glass had caused condensation or steam to appear, and the goggles had fogged up.

Harry said, "I know how to solve this." He dipped his goggles in the water. He then spat into his goggles and rubbed the spit around the glass.

"Yuck!" said Solly. "Harry, that's gross, man. You are freaking me out."

Harry looked across at Solly, feeling very pleased with himself that he had managed to gross Solly out. "No, I'm telling you, Solly; this is how you do it. I watched a video on YouTube, and this is how to stop your goggles from steaming up. I'm telling you; it's legit."

"Okay," said Solly, looking sceptically at his friend. He dipped his goggles in the water; then really sucking his breath in, he sent a huge, globular ball of spit into the inside of his diving mask. He started to wipe it around with a very distressed look on his face.

"Harry, I'm not sure I want to put this on my face," said Solly, crinkling his nose is disgust.

"Oh, don't be such as sissy," said Harry. "Come on!"

The two boys slipped on their diving goggles, and sure enough, the spit stopped the goggles from steaming up.

Soon the boys were swimming all around the pool with their snorkels or breathing tubes in their mouths. They slowly mastered the technique of breathing cleanly in and out, in and out.

Harry looked across at his friend, as Solly glided beautifully through the water. Harry swam up behind him, and without giving a warning dived onto his friend's back. Solly was pushed deep beneath the water.

Solly exploded out of the water, coughing and spitting the breathing tube out of his mouth. He looked across at Harry and said, "Man, are you crazy? What are you doing? You nearly drowned me; all the water went down my breathing tube, and I ended up with a mouthful of water."

"Solly," roared Harry with laughter, "I thought it was really, really funny."

Harry was laughing so much that he tripped over a rock on the bottom of the tidal pool. Falling onto his back, Harry disappeared right under the water. Water rushed into his breathing tube as well, and the next minute he was also coughing and spluttering.

Both boys fell against each other laughing. "That was fun," they said in unison.

All the time the boys had been playing in the tidal pool, they had not really been keeping an eye on the water beyond the rock shelf. They hadn't given much thought to the fact that the tide was coming in. If they had taken a closer look, they would have seen that the water – which previously had been at least six foot below the tidal rock shelf – was now only about four feet below. The tide was starting to come in, and the

Great White Sharks were still cruising around in the water looking for a meal. One of them would occasionally even bump up against the rock shelf, but the boys were having far too much fun to notice.

Harry came up out of the water and called across to Solly, "Solly, Solly, come look."

Solly swam across to his friend, and both of them ducked their heads under the water. The scene before them was a magnificent one. Between two big rocks swam a multitude of varied beautiful fish. One in particular was an explosion of lovely colours.

Harry put his foot out, and the fish darted away into the deep crevice between two rocks.

Harry said, "I want a closer look; let's see if I can flush it out again." He put his foot, together with his flipper, even deeper into the gap between the rocks. Still the fish did not appear, so he pushed his leg even further in – stretching as far as he could.

Suddenly, one of the big rocks moved. Harry's flipper had dislodged a small rock that was helping to balance the big rock. The big rock shifted, sending up clouds of sea sand all around it.

"Ow! Ow! Ow!" screamed Harry. "My foot is stuck between the rocks. The rocks have rolled onto it. Quickly, Solly, help me!"

Solly quickly grabbed hold of his friend and started to pull.

Harry just screamed louder and louder, crying out, "It hurt. It hurts."

The rock would not budge. Harry's foot would not budge, and Harry's ankle would not budge. He wailed again. "Help, help!" The pain could be clearly heard in his voice.

Chapter 3: Trapped

Solly looked across at his friend. Harry's face was writhing in pain, as the weight of the heavy rock pushed down onto his foot and ankle. As Solly looked down, he saw some discolouration in the water. Quickly putting on his diving mask again, he dove down into the water – which was beginning to feel deeper. There, coming off of Harry's ankle was some bright red blood, which was starting to spread in the water. It was not a lot of blood, but it was bleeding nevertheless.

Harry's ankle and foot had been cut by the shifting rock, and he was bleeding.

Solly pulled his head out of the water, took off his mask and said to his friend, who was by now leaning up against another rock and trying to pull his leg out, "Harry, stop pulling! You will just hurt yourself more. Look! You're already bleeding into the water.

"What?!" screamed Harry. "I'm losing my blood? How much of it?"

"Well, not too much," said Solly, "but enough."

"What do you mean enough?" wailed Harry. "Am I bleeding badly or not?"

"Well," said Solly, "I think you will live if we can get you out of the water, but I'm not strong enough to move that rock. I need help."

"I can't help much," said Harry. "I can hardly stand, and the pain is getting worse."

"No problem," said Solly. "Don't worry. I'll quickly run home and get Mom and Dad to come and help us"

A look of fright, followed by fear crossed Harry's face.

"I don't think that's a good idea!" he said looking over Solly's shoulder towards the open water.

"What do you mean?" said Solly. "It'll only take me about half an hour to get there, and coming back by car will probably take only ten minutes."

"*Ja*" said Harry. "That is going to be a problem, Solly. Look behind you!"

Solly turned and faced the open water. Looking across the rock shelf, he saw that the tide was in fact coming in. The water that had been six foot below the rock shelf was now less than a foot from the top of the rock shelf.

"Oh no!" said Solly. "I forgot the tide is coming in. I didn't even think to keep checking."

"No, neither did I," said Harry. "If you walk back home and then drive back, that is at least 40 minutes. Look at how quickly the water is coming in; we don't have much time."

"Look! It's already risen another inch," said Solly. "This is not good."

"No, it isn't," said Harry looking further beyond the rock shelf. "Look!"

Out in the deeper water, just off the tidal wall, big sharks were gathering.

Harry continued, "That water will soon start to come over the rock shelf. We know that it can rise to six to seven feet over the tidal wall at high tide. The sharks will soon be able to get into this tidal pool. Normally they don't come in, because they don't think there's any food here. But I am bleeding into the water! We both watched that documentary on TV. Remember, they told us that sharks are attracted to blood."

"*Ja*, I remember," said Solly. "They also said something about a shark being able to detect or identify one drop of blood in 100 litres of water and up to a distance of three miles away. They then hone in on the blood."

Harry looked down at his bleeding ankle and foot. "Yes, and there is more than one drop of blood in the water. If we don't get me out of here, and the water keeps rising, those sharks are going to be able to come in. As soon as the water is deep enough, those sharks are going to be coming for me. I'm going to be breakfast for them!"

Both little boys went absolutely quiet as the situation really dawned on them, and fear began to take hold of them.

Harry said, "Solly, we have a second problem. With the water rising, it's already at my chin."

Sure enough, the water level was rising. The incoming tide was pushing water through the cracks in the rock shelf. The water in the tidal pool was also starting to rise. Solly was okay, because he could stand up; but Harry was trapped at an angle, brought about by leaning into the crevice to try and scare the fish out. Now, he was holding onto the rock, and the water was lapping just below his chin.

Solly said, "Harry, if that water keeps rising, you're not going able to breathe."

Solly could see the fear in Harry's face. He thought for a moment, then said, "I know what we can do. Put your mask on, and breathe through your snorkel."

Harry said, "*Ja*, that'll work for a while; but even with my snorkel on, it's not going to be able to last for long. The rising tide will soon be higher than my snorkel."

Solly thought for another minute, and then he pulled off his snorkel and stuck the mouthpiece onto the top of Harry's snorkel. His clever move extended the snorkel; the two snorkels now joined together made the tube long enough for Harry to be able to breathe, even if the water rose to a metre above his head.

But that didn't solve the biggest problem. The water was coming in very quickly now; it was now less than six inches from the top of the rock shelf. Soon, the water would start to lap over the tidal wall.

"Once the water is high enough, those sharks will be coming to eat us. What are we going to do?" said Harry, his voice shaking with fear.

Chapter 4: Rescue

Solly was thinking furiously. *What could he do to save his friend?* If he left him and ran for help, he wouldn't get there in time. By the time he got back, the water would have flooded over the rock shelf and the sharks would have access to his friend.

What was he going to do? He thought furiously, sending up a prayer for his friend.

Then he said, "Harry, wait here!"

Harry looked at his friend, a wry smile on his face. He said, "Solly, I don't think I'm going anywhere. I'm stuck remember."

"Oh yes, sorry, "said Solly. Solly had thought of something. He quickly made his way back to the beach and the little backpack he had brought with him. He opened up the side pocket and took out a little mirror that he always carried with him.

Coming back to Harry, Solly said, "Look! I've got my mirror."

With a look of absolute disbelief on his face, Harry turned to his friend and said, "Solly, have you gone mad? Here we are in a desperate situation. The water is coming in, I'm bleeding blood into the water and soon, the water will be high enough for the sharks to start to coming across the rock shelf. They are going to eat me, and you are showing me your mirror!"

"No, Harry," said Solly. "You don't understand! My dad said I must always take this mirror with me. He said I can use it to call for help."

Harry wished he could reach across and grabbed hold of Solly's shoulders and give him a good shake.

"He taught me how to use this mirror to call for help," Solly continued.

Harry looked at his friend like he'd gone mad. "Solly, your mirror is not a cell phone; you can't call for help. Anyway, there are no mobile or cell towers around here."

"No, no," said Solly, "Look out on the water." There, beyond the sharks were fishing boats. The fishermen were out looking for the early morning catch, but they were too far away to hear the boys if they tried shouting.

Once again Solly said, "Just wait here!"

Harry, with a look of disbelief on his face, said "Solly, I've told you once already. I'm not going anywhere; remember... I'm stuck!"

Solly slipped off his flippers, clambered up onto the highest rock he could find and held the mirror in his hands so that he could catch the rays of the sun on it.

He started flashing out, three dots, three dashes, and three dots. Over and over again, three quick flashes of the mirror, followed by three longer flashes, followed by three shorter flashes went out. It was the international code for assistance, SOS - Save Our Souls. Solly's dad always joked and called it SOS, Save Our Sausages.

Up on the rock Solly kept flashing. Then from one of the fishing boats far out, he got an answer – the flash, flash, flash of a high-powered signalling lamp.

What Solly could not know was that out on the fishing boat, the captain had his high-powered binoculars to his eyes. He was looking out over the water. He could see the sharks, he could see the rising tide and he could see the little boy who was standing on top of the rock with his mirror flashing out the international SOS signal. He could also see there was another boy in the water, and that the water was already starting to cover his face. The captain also noticed that two snorkels had been joined together.

The sea captain quickly summed up the situation and realised that something must have happened to the boy in the water. With his high-powered binoculars, Captain Jacobs could also see that there was a sort of reddish- brownish tinge in the water.

As an experienced fisherman, he immediately identified it as blood. The captain moved across to his radio and picked up the handset. Within seconds he was in touch with the coastguard and the National Sea Rescue Institute.

Back at the tidal pool Harry was really battling to stay upright; the buffering waves were hitting him as the water started to push across the top of the tidal rock wall.

Solly saw him battling and stopped flashing with the mirror. He quickly made his way down into the pool again and tried to support Harry from the back.

As the boys were being buffeted by the waves, they suddenly heard the noise of a helicopter coming across the clear Cape sky. Within a few minutes, a big, Red helicopter with large, yellow writing proclaiming National Sea Rescue on the side door hovered overhead.

That door now opened, and a man in a red wetsuit was being winched down. Within seconds there was a man next to Solly and Harry. He said, "Hello, boys, my name is Dan. What's going on here?"

The boys quickly garbled out the whole story. Dan spoke into his radio, and soon another man came down from the helicopter bringing a big metal bar with him.

"Right," said Dan, "let's buy us some extra time." Dan then proceeded to pull out a bag full of yellow fluid from a pouch on his wetsuit. Tearing open the bag, he let the fluid pour into the water.

"Shark repellent!" Dan said to the boys. "It will not keep those big boys away for long, but it will give us at least another few minutes."

Dan instructed Solly to support Harry, while he and the other man put the big metal bar between the two rocks. The two very big, strong sea divers pushed with all their energy on the big bar, and slowly the rocks shifted. As they shifted, Harry's foot came loose; and with Solly holding him, he popped out and floated to the surface.

"Whew! Thank you so much," said Harry. "I thought I was a goner!"

Dan looked around and said, "Boys, if we don't get out of here, we are all going to be goners."

The boys look past Dan, and saw that the water had risen another metre. The Great White Sharks had already picked up the trail of blood, and they were starting to nose their way just across the top of the rock shelf. There was not yet enough water for them to make their way in, but it was rising very, very quickly; another five minutes and the water would be deep enough for the sharks to make their way across the rock shelf and attack the boys and their rescuers.

Dan quickly took hold of the harnesses that had been dropped from the helicopter, clipped the two boys into them and gave the thumbs up.

In a matter of seconds the boys were whizzing through the sky and arrived at the open door of the helicopter, where another man pulled them in and unclipped them. The harnesses were then dropped rapidly down again. Within another few minutes, the rescuers were back in the helicopter.

The helicopter moved on and hovered over the beach. Dan quickly winched his way down and picked up the boys' belongings. Once Dan was back in the helicopter, it set off at high speed towards the nearest hospital.

As the helicopter flew over the tidal pool, the boys looked down. There, just on the rock shelf, they could see the first of the sharks making its way across the rock shelf and into the tidal pool attracted by the blood that was in the water. But of course now there was nothing for them to eat.

Thanks to that little mirror and the SOS signal that the captain had seen, the boys were safe.

They zoomed over False Bay and landed at one of the Cape Town hospitals, where Harry was rushed into casualty for his wound to be assessed.

Chapter 5: Shark Cage Dive

It was one week later, and the boys were so excited.

It had turned out, after the doctor had examined Harry, that the only injury was a deep cut on his ankle. It had been stitched, and a week later the wound was already closed.

The boys were really excited; today was the day that they were going to go shark cage diving with the family.

They arrived at Simons Town Harbour at 6:00am and climbed on board the chartered boat. Before they knew it, the boat was heading out into the deep waters of False Bay, and very soon they anchored off Seal Island.

Solly and Harry's eyes scanned the water looking for a sign of the sharks. They couldn't see fins anywhere. They had been hoping for crystal clear water, but the water was a little bit murky.

"I can't see any sharks," wailed Solly.

"Oh no!" said Harry. "I hope we will not be disappointed."

The captain of the boat laughed. He said, "Trust me, boys; you can't see the sharks, but they are there nevertheless. You'll see them soon enough."

The boys, together with their moms and dads, got into their wetsuits. They then put on their aqualungs, followed by the dive masks, which they popped on top of their heads.

"Don't I look like a professional diver?" smirked Harry.

"*Ja*," said Solly. "I believe Great White Sharks like to eat professional divers!"

Harry felt a shiver go down his spine. The experiences of a week ago, when he was on the sharks' menu, were still fresh in his mind.

They were given a short briefing on safety procedures and how to breathe through the aqualung. Then, the big winch lifted two shark cages over the side.

Solly and Harry went into one cage, and Solly's dad and mom went into the other. Once they were safely in the cages, one of the fishermen sitting at the end of the boat next to a bucket of really terrible smelling stuff started to ladle the stinky brew into the water.

The mixture of offal, fish heads and blood was called chum. The fisherman began to pour it in the water, and you could see the trail of the oily mixture on the surface as it began to be carried by the current.

Within four or five minutes, a dark shape materialised out of the murky blue. Then another and another and another!

The menacing dark shapes circled around the boat and the two cages, coming closer with each revolution.

Suddenly, the dark shapes leapt into focus. They were Great White Sharks of all sizes. Not one, not two, not three... but at least a dozen sharks were moving in and out, coming closer all the time.

Bang! The cage suddenly gave a mighty lurch as a four-metre-long Great White Shark gave it a bump with its nose. Solly and Harry turned, their eyes as big as saucers, and there on the other side of the cage was a huge Great White Shark.

It was gigantic! It almost seemed to be as big as the boat that was bobbing on the surface.

"It must be almost six metres," thought Solly to himself.

The boys were mesmerised as a large shark came in at speed towards the cage; its eyes rolled back as it opened its massive jaws before locking them onto the bars of the cage. The shark started to shake its head from side to side, causing the cage to tilt and swing back and forth.

Solly and Harry went tumbling through the water along the cage floor, before stabilising themselves.

Both boys were breathing very rapidly into their respirators, a long stream of bubbles giving testimony to the fear they were experiencing.

Solly's dad held up his thumb and smiled at them, his eyes glinting with humour behind is dive mask.

Reassured, the boys started to relax. The bubbles coming from their respirators stabilised as they started to breathe normally. They realised that they were safe in the cage. Solly and Harry settled down and actually started to enjoy this wonderful experience. They felt truly blessed to be there and to see these magnificent creatures in their natural habitat. What an experience! What a day!

Chapter 6: Judgement Day

Early on Sunday morning, the day after the family outing on the shark diving expedition, the two families were together having a meal.

Solly and Harry's dads called the two boys across to them and said, "Now, boys, we need to talk; we didn't want to punish you last week, because Harry was injured, and we had the big experience of the shark cage dive coming up. But now that we've had that experience, we hope you boys have learnt how dangerous sharks can be."

Both boys nodded, remembering the fear they had felt when the shark had bitten their cage, shaking them around.

Harry's dad looked at his son and said, "Yes, young man, you could have ended up inside the tummy of one of those sharks for doing what you did. Going off without telling us where you were going and what you were doing was not very wise."

Solly's dad looked across at him and said, "Solly, you did very well to call for help with your mirror, BUT you also know that it was not right to go off without telling me or mom where you were going."

The two little boys hung their heads. "We're sorry; we just didn't think."

"Precisely," said Harry's dad, "and that can be a problem. Sometimes, when you do things without thinking, you put yourself in very real danger."

"Yes, Sir," said both boys in unison.

"Right, boys; this is your punishment." said Solly's dad. "For the next two Saturdays, you boys are going to be painting the fence outside of our two houses."

"Oh no!" said the two boys. "That's not fair. Saturday is our day off from school. It's the only day when we can go and have some adventure and fun."

Harry's dad said sternly, "Well, boys, you had an adventure, and you had some fun... but you were also very naughty. You need to learn that you can't always go off and do what you want."

"Yes, okay," said the two now very subdued boys.

The next Saturday, the two boys were busy painting the fence, reliving the adventure of the shark encounter.

Solly looked across at Harry and said, "Harry, I was so scared!"

Harry answered and said, "You and I both, Solly. I was also really scared – both in the tidal pool and in the shark cage. Those sharks are awesome! Remember on the way back, when one came out of the water – the guide called it 'breaching' – and took that seal for lunch. Man, I got such a fright! I won't tell you how much of a fright I got; it's too embarrassing. But it was awesome to see the sharks.

"*Ja*," said Solly. "Now, when we have finished painting this fence, we've also got to write in our journal. Mr Abrahams, our headmaster, also heard about our adventure. He wants us to add another page to our journal about the things that we have learnt on our shark encounter."

The End

Solly and Harry-Our Journal of Lessons Learnt.

Solly and Harry's Journal.

1. Always tell your parents where you are going.
2. Always think before you do something. Ask yourself
   - Is this right?
   - Is it safe?
   - Would my parents be happy?
3. In an emergency, don't panic. Stay calm and seek help.
4. Always plan an adventure and make sure you have the right equipment.

Post Script

For a free audio copy of this book please email caracalbooks@caracalbooks.org with *Solly-Shark* as the subject line.

An email to the audio file will be sent to you.

Coming Soon!
The Amazing Adventures of Solly and Harry – Parachuting

Other books in this series
The Amazing Adventures of Solly and Harry – Up, Up and Away

Author Website
www.greghibbinsbooks.uk

Lightning Source UK Ltd.
Milton Keynes UK
UKOW01f2312150817
307391UK00001B/29/P